Happy Birthday, Coco Bear
A Story of a Covid-born Baby Bear

Mary Lou Guthrie McDonough
Illustrations by Lisa Lyman Adams

Bumblebee Books
London

A CIP catalogue record for this title is
available from the British Library.

ISBN: 978-1-83934-373-5

Bumblebee Books is an imprint of
Olympia Publishers.

First Published in 2022

Bumblebee Books
Tallis House
2 Tallis Street
London
EC4Y 0AB

Printed in Great Britain

www.olympiapublishers.com

Dedication

I dedicate this book to my husband, Bill, our children: Will, Stephanie, Elizabeth, Dave, John, and Paula and to our grandchildren: John, Calvin, Conor, Claire, Eloise, and especially to Maggie and Bo who were born during the coronavirus and inspired this story.

I thank Lisa Adams for making *Coco Bear* come alive. Blessings to Jean and my Westwood Covid Cave friends who suggested this book be written. Thank you, Laura Connell – librarian extraordinaire.

Foreward

Coco Bear is a bear born during the coronavirus of 2020. Family traditions of welcoming a new baby were suspended and new ones took their place. Join Coco Bear and the Bear family on Coco Bear's birthday when the restrictions of the virus are lifted.

"Happy birthday, Scout Bear," said Daddy Bear. "It's your special day! We will have our family and friends come to play and open presents. But first, let's have our traditional birthday breakfast. Put on your birthday hat and get ready for the pancakes."

At breakfast, as was their tradition, Scout Bear, Mommy Bear, Daddy Bear, and Coco Bear all looked at pictures of the day Scout Bear was born.

Scout Bear wore a cone shaped birthday hat at breakfast and kept it on all day.

"Here are pictures of the day you were born, Scout Bear," said Daddy Bear.

They all looked at the pictures of Grandma Bear holding Scout Bear, while Grandpa Bear, Grammy Bear, and Papa Bear all smiled proudly.

"Look at all the balloons and gifts!" said Scout Bear.

"Your cousins, aunts, and uncles were all excited to meet you," said Mommy Bear as she pointed to another picture.

"Look at us, Daddy Bear," said Mommy Bear. "We are so proud and happy holding our new bundle of love surrounded by our family and so much excitement."

"It looks like a fun party!" exclaimed Scout Bear. "There are my cousins, John, Calvin, Conor, Claire, Eloise, Maggie, and Bo!"

Coco Bear loved seeing all of the gifts, balloons, and the hospital room full of happy faces. "I can't wait to see my party pictures when it's my birthday," said Coco Bear.

Mommy Bear and Daddy Bear looked at each other. Mommy Bear picked up Coco Bear and said, "We were all so happy the day you were born, too!"

A few months later, it was Coco Bear's birthday. Mommy Bear, Daddy Bear, and Scout Bear went to Coco Bear's bed with a crown to place on Coco Bear's head.

'Hmm,' thought Coco Bear. 'This is different from the birthday hat that Scout Bear wore, but I like it.'

As they ate breakfast, Coco Bear could not wait to see the birthday pictures of the party in the hospital.

Mommy Bear and Daddy Bear took out the pictures. "Look at us, Coco Bear. Daddy Bear and I are so happy to be holding you."

"But, are you sure that's you, Mommy Bear and Daddy Bear?" Coco Bear asked. "I only see your eyes."

"That's because when you were born, it was during the coronavirus and we all had to wear masks so we did not spread germs."

"Here we are sitting on the bed together," said Daddy Bear.

"But, where are Grammy Bear, Grandpa Bear, Grandma Bear, and Papa Bear? Where are my cousin bears, my aunt bears, and my uncle bears? Where are the balloons? Where are the presents?" asked Coco Bear.

"You were born during the coronavirus. That's why we called you Coco Bear. None of your grandparents, aunts, uncles, or cousins were allowed to visit. They all agreed to stay away to protect you from getting sick from the virus because they love you so much," said Mommy Bear.

"We needed to keep you safe. You were our special baby we had all to ourselves. The best we could do was show you off to everyone using our laptop and iPad."

"Even Scout Bear had to wait until you came home to meet you. Mommy Bear and Daddy Bear were alone with you in the hospital for two days. Even though you only see our eyes, you could feel our love as we held you and called you Coco Bear. Our special coronavirus baby! You, Daddy Bear, and I had made our own party of three," explained Mommy Bear.

Daddy Bear adjusted the crown on Coco Bear's head. "It is YOUR tradition to wear a crown on you head at your birthday because corona means 'crown'."

"But, today", said Mommy Bear, "we are having a BIG party with ALL of our family and you will see ALL of our faces, you will have lots of balloons and gifts to open."

Coco Bear turned around to see Daddy Bear with balloons in one hand and brightly wrapped presents in the other. Coco Bear laughed and adjusted the crown.

Coco Bear said, "I am a special coco-virus bear. We are all safe from the virus now, but I will wear my crown forever!"

About the Author

Dr. Mary Lou Guthrie McDonough has been a special educator for over forty years. She earned her doctorate in special education at Boston University, holds degrees from Harvard University, Rhode Island College and Lesley University. She has worked at several Boston universities. She has been a teacher of children with special needs and an inclusion specialist. She is founder and president of Educational Consultants of Boston. She has been married to her husband Bill for over forty years. Mary Lou is the proud mother of Will, Stephanie, Elizabeth, Dave, John, Paula and grandmother to John, Calvin, Conor, Claire, Eloise, Maggie and Bo.

Acknowledgements

I wish to thank my family for encouraging and helping me with this book. I thank Lisa Adams who made Coco Bear come alive. Blessings to Jean and my Westwood friends who suggested the book be written.